Jesus, Do You Want to Be My Friend?

First edition. June 9, 2019.

Written by Mark Restaino.

Jesus, Do You Want to Be My Friend?

Illustrations by JP Alcomendas
Story by Mark Restaino

Who are some of your friends?

One of my friends is Jesus. Jesus was once a child just like you. Jesus played and had fun just like you and your friends do.

One really nice thing about my friend Jesus is that he can always hear me. Whenever I want to talk to him, I just close my eyes, ask him questions, and listen for answers. Isn't that cool?

Well guess what?! Jesus wants to be your friend too!

That means you can talk to him and ask him questions whenever you want to.

These are some questions that we can ask Jesus.

Jesus, can you help me get up?

"I can do all things through Christ who gives me strength."
Philippians 4:13

Jesus, can you teach me how to fish?

"Come after me, and I will make you fishers of men."
Matthew 4:19

Jesus, can you show me what it means to be obedient?

"If you keep my commandments, you will remain in my love,
just as I have kept my Father's commandments
and remain in his love."
John 15:10

Jesus, can you heal me?

"Thus says the Lord, the God of David your father:
I have heard your prayer; I have seen your tears.
Now I am healing you."
2 Kings 20:5

Jesus, how can I ever thank you enough?

"Give thanks to the Lord for he is good,
his mercy endures forever!"
Psalm 107:1

Jesus, can you help me forgive?

"Be kind to one another, compassionate, forgiving one another
as God has forgiven you in Christ."
Ephesians 4:32

Jesus, can you find me?

"Where can I go from your spirit?
From your presence, where can I flee?"
Psalm 139:7

Jesus, can you take the lead?

"Trust in the Lord with all your heart
and lean not on your own understanding."
Proverbs 3:5

Jesus, can you take care of my friend?

"The Lord watches over all who love him."
Psalm 145:20

Jesus, can you teach me how to see the world differently?

"Thus, the last will be first, and the first will be last."
Matthew 20:16

Jesus, can you wash this clean?

"If we acknowledge our sins, he is faithful and just
and will forgive our sins
and cleanse us from every wrongdoing."
1 John 1:9

Jesus, can you bring forth some good fruit?

"I am the vine, you are the branches. Whoever remains in me and I in him will bear much fruit, because without me you can do nothing."
John 15:5

Jesus, will you provide for me?

"Therefore I tell you, do not worry about your life,
what you will eat or drink, or about your body, what you will wear.
Is not life more than food and the body more than clothing?
Look at the birds in the sky; they do not sow or reap,
they gather nothing into barns,
yet your heavenly Father feeds them.
Are not you more important than they?"
Matthew 6:25-26

Jesus, can you show me how to be at peace?

"Come to me, all you who labor and are burdened,
and I will give you rest."
Matthew 11:28

Jesus, can you walk beside me?

"And behold, I am with you always, until the end of the age."
Matthew 28:20

Jesus, do you love me?

"No one has greater love than this,
to lay down one's life for one's friends."
John 15:13

Jesus, can you protect me?

"Even though I walk through the valley of the shadow of death,
I will fear no evil, for you are with me;
your rod and your staff comfort me."
Psalm 23:4

Jesus, can you show me how to be joyful always?

"Consider it all joy, my brothers,
when you encounter various trials,
for you know that the testing of your faith
produces perseverance."
James 1:2–3

Jesus, can I sing a song for you?

"Sing to the Lord a new song;
sing to the Lord, all the earth.
Sing to the Lord, bless his name;
proclaim his salvation day after day.
Tell his glory among the nations;
among all peoples, his marvelous deeds."
Psalm 96:1–3

Jesus, can you hear me?

"As for me, I call to God,
and the Lord saves me.
Evening, morning and noon
I cry out in distress,
and he hears my voice."
Psalm 55:16–17

Jesus, can you help me swim in deep waters?

"Do not fear, for I have redeemed you;
I have called you by name: you are mine.
When you pass through waters, I will be with you;
through rivers, you shall not be swept away."
Isaiah 43:1-2

Jesus, how can I help you build your kingdom?

"As each one has received a gift, use it to serve one another as good stewards of God's varied grace."
1 Peter 4:10

Jesus, can you teach me how to do that?

"Humble yourselves before the Lord and he will exalt you."
James 4:10

Jesus, can you guide me home?

"In my Father's house there are many dwelling places.
If there were not, would I have told you that
I am going to prepare a place for you?
And if I go and prepare a place for you, I will come back again
and take you to myself, so that where I am you also may be."
John 14:2-3

Jesus, can you shed some light on this?

"Your word is a lamp for my feet,
a light for my path."
Psalm 119:105

Jesus, can you tell me a good story?

"For God so loved the world that he gave his one and only Son, that whoever believes in him shall not perish but have eternal life."
John 3:16

God, can we be friends forever?

Pleeease?

MARK RESTAINO

SYMBOLICALLY SHARING THE FAITH AND GOSPEL MESSAGE

I am a full time youth minister and live in the Chicagoland area with my wife and two daughters.

I got the idea for my first story while on a retreat with my youth group students. My other stories also seem to come to me in the quiet moments when I reflect on my life and faith.

I am personally drawn to the symbolism and foreshadowing that God weaves throughout the Bible and I believe it serves as beautiful defense of the faith.

In reflection of my creator, I strive to write stories that capture readers' hearts and minds and symbolically share the faith and gospel message.

I pray that my stories kindle the fire of the faith within you, your family, and your church community.

Thank you for your support.

THANK YOU FOR YOUR SUPPORT

LEVEL I

Leave an honest review for this book on Amazon.

LEVEL II

Follow me on Facebook and Instagram and subscribe to my email newsletter.

facebook.com/authormarkrestaino
@authormarkrestaino
authormarkrestaino.com

LEVEL III

Join my beta reader team, review team, or influencer team at authormarkrestaino.com/teams.

LEVEL IV

Place half price bulk orders of my books for gifts or fundraisers at authormarkrestaino.com/order.

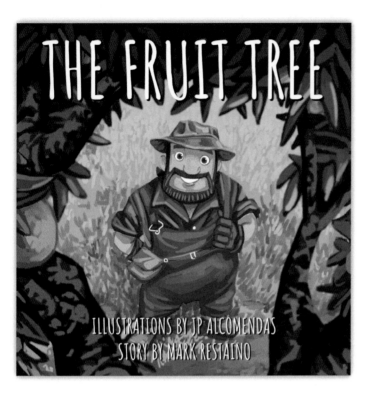

Plant the gospel seed within your children and watch it grow.

This beautifully illustrated children's book features a gardener, his fruit tree, a plot against them, and their blooming forgiveness to tell a symbolic gospel story.

Allegorical animals and objects are woven throughout the narrative and explained in the back of the book.

In addition, Bible verses, displayed in the corner of each image, walk the reader through the story as well as the gospel message.

Why would parents want their children to fail?

No matter how much we try, we can't protect our children from every negative experience. So instead of shielding them from difficulties, we should be instilling in our children the wisdom to turn to God whenever they experience life's trials.

This children's book contains a lineup of backward blessings paired with cute illustrations that show how God works in our suffering.

Read this book while simultaneously praying these blessings over your children.

What is your child worth?

The world is constantly shouting at and telling your child that their value and importance is determined by their looks, talents, and intelligence.

But God is whispering to them a different story. "No matter what, you are priceless."

There Once Was a Penny is a rhyming children's book that follows a penny through the hands of her three different owners as she seeks meaning and happiness and eventually finds it in the wishful words of a little girl.

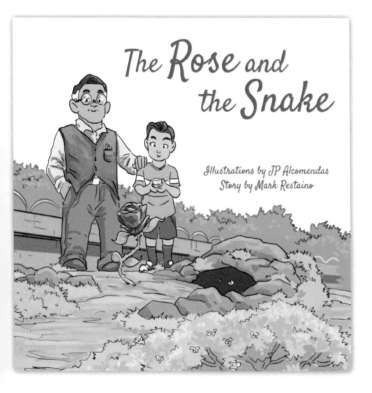

Am I beautiful? Am I loved?

These are the two questions that little girls are always thinking about. And from family and friends to magazines and billboards, the answers are endless. But there is only one response that matters.

This children's book is a biblically symbolic story of a rose who is manipulated by a snake, struggles with her appearance, and eventually finds her confidence in the wise words of a compassionate boy.

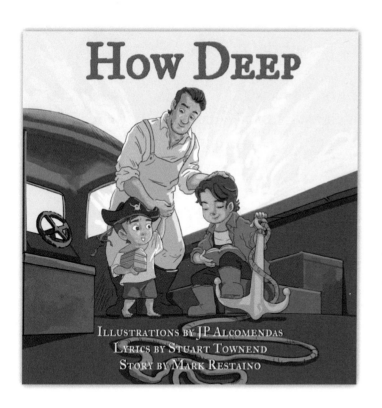

Sing along and worship with your children and watch as a gospel story unfolds.

Synced with the lyrics of "How Deep the Father's Love For Us" by Stuart Townend, the illustrations in this book tell the story of a father, his two sons, and an eventful trip at sea.

This story will grab your heart and serve as a special way for you to communicate the gospel to your children.

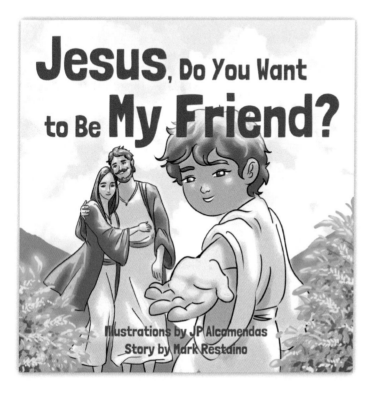

Have you ever pictured Jesus Christ climbing trees, dancing in the rain, or playing hide and seek?

This children's book follows our young Savior through a day full of fun. Prayers in the form of questions along with Bible verse responses make this one of those perfect stories to read to your children right before they go to bed as it will inspire them to reflect on their day and be thankful for the friend they have in Jesus.

Give your children prayers that they can picture in their hearts and minds to strengthen their relationship with Jesus Christ.

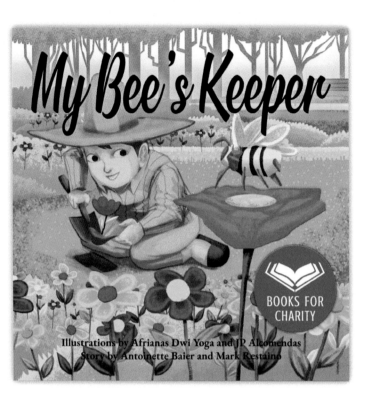

Make your child's day bright and sunny with this book about grace and honey.

This sweet and rhyming children's book features a family in need, a friendly gardener, and the life giving power of bees to tell a symbolic gospel story. The book touches on the topics of homelessness, immigration, the environment, and of course, the Christian faith.

Another great thing about this book is that all net author proceeds are donated to Christian organizations that house the homeless, refugees, and missionaries.

Why do bad things happen if God loves me?

This symbolic gospel story introduces families to two child-like robots. One has the ability to choose and the other is only able to do good.

Through unconditional love, mercy, and forgiveness, this tale answers the age-old problem of evil in a way both parents and children will understand.

Instill this truth in your children:
No matter what you do, God will always love you.

Made in the USA
Columbia, SC
17 December 2019